Making Reading Fun!

Chrysalis Children's Books

For Mishti, Robene and Sanjee - HB

For Sushila, Terry and Sue - RJ

First published in
Great Britain in 2004 by
Chrysalis Children's Books
an imprint of Chrysalis Books Group plc
The Chrysalis Building, Bramley Road
London W10 6SP
www.chrysalisbooks.co.uk
This paperback edition first published in 2005

Text copyright © 2004 Henriette Barkow
Illustration copyright © 2004 Richard Johnson

The moral right of the author and illustrator
has been asserted.

Designed by Sarah Goodwin

BRITISH LIBRARY CATALOGUING-IN-PUBLICATION DATA
A catalogue record for this book is available
from the British Library.

ISBN 1 85602 519 5 (hardback)
ISBN 1 84458 056 3 (paperback)
Printed in China

If Elephants Wore Trousers...

Henriette Barkow

Illustrated by
Richard Johnson

Chrysalis Children's Books

If elephants wore trousers,
what trousers would they wear?

Would they be fluffy and pink,
like my big sister's pair?

Or would they be velvety brown, like the fur of a bear?

Would they be rainbow-speckled,
like the clowns' at the fair?

Or would they be dappled and green,
like the skin of a pear?

If elephants wore trousers,
what trousers would they wear?

Would they be blue and crisp,
like the frosty night air?

Or would they be sunflower yellow, like grandpa's old chair?

Would they be
crackling and red,
like a ship's mighty flare?

Or would they be shimmering gold,
like the beads in Mum's hair?

If elephants wore trousers,

do you know what they'd wear?

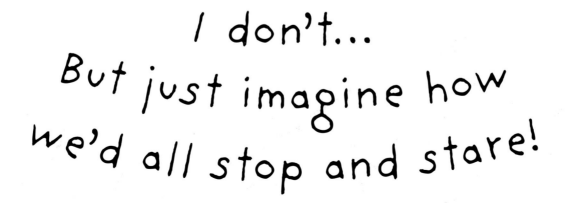

I don't...
But just imagine how
we'd all stop and stare!

More fun books for you to read!

ISBN 1 84365 056 8

ISBN 1 84458 140 3 (pb)

ISBN 1 84365 061 4

ISBN 1 84365 026 6 (hb)
ISBN 1 84458 157 8 (pb)

ISBN 1 84365 025 8

ISBN 1 84365 017 7